The Erotic Adventures of a Victorian Doctor: The Countess' Role Play Fantasies

Dorian Shellan

CONTENTS

1 Spanking the Countess

In the two years he had been in practice, Doctor Damian Thatch had built an impressive clientele of ladies from London's upper class. Most of them came to his consulting room to be treated for hysteria or malaise, yet only a few recognized, or at least were willing to admit the fact, that the paroxysm he induced through pelvic massage was actually a sexual orgasm. The Countess Cynthia of Sagadonia was one of those few.

Lady Cynthia was a most attractive woman of twenty six with a fine brunette complexion, hazel eyes, and a pair of full formed breasts. Unabashed in her understanding of the true nature of pelvic massage, she was prone to writhing and audible abandon during her treatments. This invariably provided Damian with a most unprofessional arousal as he ministered to her, but he always succeeded in maintaining the outward appearance of physician's detachment. This was the reason why he always scheduled the countess as his last consultation for the day, following which he would have his dolly mop maid, Rosie, attend to him.

The countess, of course, was completely unaware of the tension she created within Damian's pants. Neither would she have cared. As a member of the aristocracy, she was above Damian's social station and merely considered him as the provider of a service. There would be no small talk, and she simply paid him his guinea fee on her way out.

During today's session, however, Lady Cynthia's response to Damian's manual dexterity was particularly exuberant. At the critical juncture of supreme pleasure, her whole spirit seemed to dissolve within her. Her trembling lips released screams of delight as she descended into throes of pleasure until she seemed to melt into quiet satisfaction. As Damian slowly withdrew his right hand from beneath her dress, the countess remained lying down on Damian's couch, relishing in afterglow. He sat quietly on the edge of the couch next to her until her hazel eyes fluttered to indicate she had sufficiently recovered. Rather than make an attempt to rise, however, the countess remained reposed on the couch and spoke to him. "Tell me doctor," she began. "Are you familiar with the current fascination ladies have with reading novels?"

"Indeed I am, Lady Cynthia." Damian was delighted to engage her in conversation, something she had never done before. "In fact, several of my patients have made mention to me of the pleasures they derive from them."

"I, too, am finding them to be wonderful diversions. Of course," she almost smiled, "My husband, the earl, considers them to be trivial and quite innocent. So he remains unaware of how they provide such a curious arousal of the senses."

"Most gentlemen share that same attitude towards novels, Countess. Clearly, it is the ladies such as yourself who are causing them to gain so much in popularity."

"Indeed. But I am of late finding that some subject matter causes me to take pause."

"How so?"

"There is much written about spanking and flogging." Lady Cynthia sat up as she spoke. "Tell me doctor, are you aware of people actually becoming aroused while receiving discipline?"

"Very much so." Damian smiled reassuringly. "In fact, in mainland Europe the desire for spanking is often referred to as the English vice."

"Then I must confide a secret to you, doctor." She looked askance. "If I may."

"But of course, Lady Cynthia," Doctor Thatch responded casually. "And be assured that nothing you share with me will ever leave this room."

"I was thinking about being spanked while you were providing my treatment today. I found it both enhanced the process and had a profound effect upon the outcome."

"Have you ever been spanked, my lady?"

"A long time ago, before I was married. I lived then in my father's great house on Hanover Square. Whenever my parents were away, which was most of the time, my governess, Miss Forbes, had complete charge over the entire household. She was a strict disciplinarian, and frequently disciplined both me and the chamber maids for even the most minor of infractions."

"What form of punishment did Miss Forbes prefer to administer?"

"Spankings and floggings, primarily. Since I was no longer a child, she had converted my old nursery into her special room where she doled out punishments. I have never told anyone this, but to me it was a very exciting room. In the center of the room there was a spanking horse, and on one wall hung a collection of canes, straps and whips."

Damian permitted his expression to open to a smile, the description of Miss Forbes' punishment room being so similar to his own library upstairs. "Were you ever flogged?" He asked.

"Not flogged, no. Miss Forbes was in the hire of an aristocratic family who would dismiss her should she employ any semblance of brutality or place even the smallest scar on her charge. Unfortunately, those implements were therefore only used on the house staff. She took in a thoughtful breath. When it was determined that I was in need of discipline, my punishment would consist of either a paddling or a sound spanking. Miss Forbes was exceedingly skillful in the delivery of both."

"How so?"

"Well, her paddle was a well-oiled, flexible leather strap on a wooden handle which was beautifully wrapped in leather." Lady Cynthia beamed as she made the recollection. "It would sting like the very devil, but was guaranteed to not bruise or leave any sort of mark."

"Yet a paddling did cause you to become sexually aroused?"

"Indeed." Lady Cynthia blushed and slightly turned away, "But not so much as when I was spanked."

"And why was that?"

"When Miss Forbes determined that my punishment was to be a spanking she combined it with anticipation and humiliation. For the two hours before I was to be spanked, I was required to wear a short skirt without stockings and walk around the house. This meant that my legs were exposed to the chamber maids." Her face suddenly began to blush. "And to Joseph, our butler."

"Really? And how did this make you feel?"

"While Miss Forbes intended my humiliation to be part of my punishment, it actually aroused me. So much so, that the subsequent spanking provided me with, shall we say, a source of immense pleasure?" She looked directly at Damian. "I was recalling one of those spankings during today's pelvic massage, doctor. And I am sure you noticed the effect."

Damian smiled as he tried to ignore the pulsing sensations in his pants. "And as you have discovered from your reading, you are not alone in deriving pleasure from humiliation and punishment."

"Yes. And I find it most reassuring that my fetish is shared by others." She looked coyly at Damian. "Tell me, doctor. Do you ever discipline your household servants with spanking?"

"On occasion, I do find it necessary to spank Rosie, my maid. Yes."

"Then, if I may be so bold to request it, will you consent to spanking me as a prelude to our next session?"

Damian's cock felt as if it were about to explode. "You make a rather unusual request, Lady Cynthia." He blurted out as he squirmed into a crossed leg position and regained his composure. "But it would be my pleasure to do so."

A fortnight later, the Countess Cynthia arrived at Dr. Thatch's consulting room carrying a large leather satchel, which she held up as soon as the door closed behind her. "If you will permit, Doctor Thatch, I would like to change before you initiate my spanking."

"Certainly." Damian smirked, suspecting what may be contained within the satchel, and beckoned to the screen across the other side of the room while he settled into his chair.

Only a few minutes passed before Lady Cynthia emerged and presented herself at attention in front of him. She clasped her hands behind her back and looked down, her legs pressed firmly together. She was wearing a navy blue one-piece sailor dress, the pleated hem of which reached only as far as the middle of her thighs. Her pale legs were quite bare except for white ankle socks and black buckle shoes. "This is the humiliation outfit that Miss Forbes made me wear for my spankings," she explained.

"And you were required to wear this in front of the house staff?"

"Yes. I was."

"And doing so excited you?"

"Curiously, it did," she replied. "I know everyone in the household was looking at me, and I was particularly conscious of that fact when I ascended the stairs or moved my arms." She demurely raised her hands above her head, which caused the hem to lift and expose her white drawers. "Like this. Do you see?"

"I do." It was clear to Damian how much Lady Cynthia was enjoying herself, so he decided to enhance her play by taking her to his private room to deliver her spanking. "I would like to suggest that we go upstairs, my lady, in order to proceed. I believe you will find what is in my library to be most consistent with your desire."

Damian held the door open and beckoned for Lady Cynthia to walk in front of him. She proceeded slowly up

the stairs, then stopped at the top
landing and looked back over her right
shoulder to Damian. "Joseph, our
butler, used to look up my little
dress like that, too," she said with a
most unladylike, almost impish,
giggle. "And I admit that I liked it
when he did."

"Then you are truly deserving of
your spanking," Damian responded as he
moved past her to open the library
door. "I suggest you go right away to
the spanking horse."

Lady Cynthia's eyes widened with
delight as they entered the room, and
she immediately made for the horse.
Without waiting for instruction, she
stood at one end and leaned across it
with her arms stretched out ahead of
her. Damian silently attached the
leather restraints to each of her
wrists to hold her firmly in place,
then stood behind her. "Since you
assumed the position prior to removing
your drawers," he said. "I shall be
required to take them off for you."

"Please do, doctor," she said, her
words beginning to tremble.

Damian slowly lifted up the hem of

her dress and placed it across her back. His cock stained against the confines of his pants as he reached around her waist to unfasten the ribbon holding her white cotton drawers up, and he then took a step back to watch them float to the floor around her ankles. She had perfect thighs and the most inviting alabaster bottom. Suppressing prurient thoughts regarding his own pleasure, Damian reached down to completely remove her underwear. It took his utmost concentration to remind himself that he was, after all, simply a physician providing this spanking as a warm up before inducing a medical paroxysm.

Lady Cynthia obediently raised her feet as Damian tapped her respective calves in order to free her ankles from her drawers. He then dragged his fingertips up the backs of her naked legs until his hands were in contact with those inviting buttocks. Her cheeks were firm and tight in anticipation. He lightly massaged them, and then moved to her left side before firmly bringing his right hand down onto her left buttock. The audible slap was instantly followed by a gasp emanating from the countess's

mouth. Damian proceeded slowly, but
after delivering a dozen evenly
distributed spanks to produce a rosy
patina across her entire bottom he
increased the frequency until he had
reached a staccato. Lady Cynthia
strained against the restraints and
her head began flipping from side to
side. "Now, doctor. Please," she
gasped between loud, open mouthed
pants. "Make me cum now."

She spread her legs apart and
Damian immediately şlid his right hand
between them, roughly invading her
curly bush with his fingers. Lady
Cynthia's entire body turned rigid at
the instant his fingertips made
contact with her throbbing clitoris,
and she continued to moan in pleasure
as he proceed to massage her with
well-practiced dexterity. When her
body finally fell limpid across the
horse, he removed his soaked hand and
massaged her emanated fluid into the
cheeks of her hot buttocks to help
cool them down. His cock was aching,
and Damian would gladly have forgone
his guinea fee if he could take this
beauty right then and there, but such
release for himself was not an option
with a countess. However, from that

moment on, Damian began to develop an almost insatiable desire to take his pleasure with this lady, fantasizing about having her bound helplessly before him while he entered her from behind. Would she, in future sessions, reveal more of her desires and by so doing compromise herself to where he might be able to bring this to fruition? He resolved to do his utmost to encourage her.

2 Fellatio Dreams

Lady Cynthia was clearly distracted when she arrived for her next appointment. So much so that Damian took the bold step of asking if she would like to sit a while and discuss what might be troubling her, before her session began.

"Thank you doctor," she began as she sank into a chair. "I have of late been disturbed by inner demons in the form of erotic dreams."

"What is it about these dreams that disturbs you so, Lady Cynthia?"

"They are so explicit. So much so that when I wake I cannot help but feel immoral for even having had such thoughts."

"In spite of conventional wisdom to the contrary, it is my opinion that such dreams occur to provide a healthy outlet for frustration. Is there a common theme in your dreams?"

Lady Cynthia blushed profusely and stared at her hands, clasped tightly together in her lap. "Yes," she whispered. "They always involve Joseph, the butler at my father's house." She bit her lower lip before slowly raising her eyes. "Do I horrify you, doctor?"

"Not at all." Damian smiled and slowly moved his head from side to side. "And please do not take offense at this next question, my lady. But has there ever been anything inappropriate between you and the butler, Joseph?"

"Heavens, no. Never." Her snapped response was almost indignant.

"It's all right, my lady." Damian raised his right hand. "I simply needed to exclude the obvious."

"Remember my social position,

doctor."

"Of course." Damian took a short
breath. "What you are experiencing is
a condition called erotomania. It is
the result of a depression of the mind
brought about by a conflict between
desire and morality."

"I have heard of that doctor." Her
concern was obvious. "But I have also
heard that the treatment for such a
malady can be harsh, possibly even
requiring incarceration for a time."

"That no longer needs to be the
case, Lady Cynthia," Damian spoke
reassuringly. "In fact, according to
my colleague, Dr. Rayner of St Thomas
Hospital, conditions such as yours may
be best resolved without such
treatment as you have heard about.
They can even be dealt with on out-
patient basis."

"Are you able to provide such a
remedy, doctor?" Lady Cynthia was
anxious.

"Indeed, I am fully qualified to do
so. The inner demons you make
reference to are simply symptoms. That
you have such dreams tells us that

there exists a part of your true self that you are denying. Once we discover what that is, then your demons will go away."

"How is such a discovery to be made?"

"We will re-visit incidents from your past that may serve as trigger points. If you are able, I would like you to recall any incident, no matter how minor, where something Joseph did might have evoked an erotic feeling in you."

"Now that you mention it, there may be something like that to which I bore witness. But that was many years ago, and I am afraid that I scarcely remember what it might be. Sometimes when I awake I try to hold on to the dream, but it fades away quickly as I become fully awake."

"Do not fret, Lady Cynthia. There is a technique which is very beneficial in clearing the fog surrounding memory. It is called hypnosis. Would you permit me to apply this procedure to you?"

"What would I need to do?"

"Just lean back on the couch, close your eyes, and listen to my voice. Would you like to try?"

"Yes, I would. Please proceed, doctor."

Lady Cynthia followed Damian's instruction and Damian began to speak in a low, slow tone. "Now Countess, you are at your parent's house. Tell me about it."

"It is a beautiful, big house. I can see the lovely gardens through the living room window."

"Tell me about Joseph, your family butler."

"He is such a handsome, good looking man. And so kind, too. Mother always has him accompany me whenever I want to go into town, and he always carries my packages back for me and tells me stories."

"You are back home from a shopping trip now. Can you still see Joseph?"

"Yes, he is going into his butler's pantry. He spends a lot of time there."

"What does he do in his pantry?"

"I don't know."

"Do you want to know?"

"I do. But when I sneak up to the pantry door there is a key in the lock so I cannot look through the keyhole."

"Are you able to find another way?"

"Yes. I go into the passageway behind the pantry because I know of a small window back there."

"Are you able to see through this window?"

"I try, but it is too high for me."

"What do you do?"

"I carry a stool with me into the passageway and stand on it. Now I can look through the window and see what is going on."

"What do you see?"

"Joseph is sitting at his desk and looking at a book. But wait, someone is coming into the room. It's Lucy, one of the housemaids. Joseph is pulling her to his side and showing her something in the book."

"Can you hear what they are saying?"

"No, the window is closed. But I push on the glass and it opens a crack, and I can now hear them. Lucy is laughing at one of the pictures in the book and, oh my, Joseph is trying to put his hand up her dress."

"How does Lucy respond?"

"She slaps his hand down and says that she cannot today, but perhaps she can tomorrow. Joseph says never mind, and he takes her hand in his and places it onto his lap. Now the two of them are unbuttoning Joseph's trousers together, and Joseph takes out his cock. It's all hard and stiff with a big purple head on it. Lucy is wrapping her hand around the shaft and she's rubbing it up and down. What? Joseph just put his hand on the back of Lucy's head and forced it down. He is making Lucy take the bulb of his cock into her mouth."

"How does Lucy respond to this?"

"She seems eager to do what Joseph wants and she lets him push her head back and forth. Joseph is leaning back in his chair and panting hard. Oh, he's suddenly stopped moving, it looks like he's frozen. He's let go of Lucy's head but she's still sliding his cock in and out of her mouth." Lady Cynthia began to pant. "I must get down from the stool and rush off to my room."

"You are going to return to my consulting room when I snap my fingers," Damian told her. "And when you awake, you will remember everything you have just observed."

Damian snapped his fingers and the first words from Lady Cynthia's mouth were, "My heavens! How could I have forgotten having been witness to such a thing?"

"Memories are often repressed when they cause conflict," Damian told her. "Perhaps it was due to Joseph's actions being in contrast to your predetermined opinion of him. Or, perhaps, it was being witness to the act of fellatio itself." Damian grasped Lady Cynthia's trembling left hand to comfort her. "Tell me now, while it is still fresh in your mind. What do you think this incident means to you?"

"I, I'm not sure. I just wake up from my dreams feeling tormented, and..." Her eyes suddenly widened and she placed her hands on each side of her open mouth. "Oh dear," she murmured, slowly shaking her head.

"What is it?"

"In my dreams..." Lady Cynthia slid her right hand across her mouth, then blurted out, "In my dreams, I am Lucy."

"And how does that make you feel?"

"I am aroused by it." Lady Cynthia bit her lower lip and looked away. "But I also feel so ashamed," she whispered.

"And it is your shame of being aroused by this act than no doubt has caused you to repress the memory. But do you not ever perform fellatio, now that you are married?"

"Certainly not." Her response was sharp, but it wasn't an admonishment. "That is not an activity permitted for an aristocrat." She looked up at Damian. "Is it?" Her response faded into an embarrassed whisper. "Do you think that my having that dream means that I might want to do that?"

"You already know the answer to that question, Lady Cynthia." Damian controlled his breathing and managed to maintain his professionalism in spite of a familiar pressure building against the inside of his trousers.

"What can I do, Doctor?" She asked in an impassioned voice.

"Why not discuss this with the earl? Don't you think he might respond positively to your offering him pleasure in this manner?"

"Heaven's no. He'd have me sent to an asylum for sure if I were to even suggest it. He would consider me as a prostitute if I told him I wanted to do, um, that." Her whole body shuddered. "No. He must never know that I suffer from this terrible desire." Her eyes looked pleadingly to Damian. "But you, doctor. You are the only one who knows what I must do. What I need to do." She stumbled over her words. "Would you? I cannot ask another."

Damian fought to maintain his composure as he realized what it was that the lady desired. "You must verbalize your need, Lady Cynthia," he told her, as calmly as he was able. "Let it out."

"Please may I?" Her eyes were affixed on her left hand, which was now sliding across Damian's thigh. She began to pant as she began to release herself to her desire.

"May you...?" Damian responded, instinctively allowing his legs to part at her touch. He reached out and stroked the side of her face. "You have to tell me what you want. You have to explicitly say it."

"Please may I suck your cock?" Lady Cynthia's face was blushing crimson, but her eyes were affixed on the bulge in front of her.

"Yes, my lady," he said affirmatively. "You may."

Damian felt the perspiration forming on his brow while he uneasily watched Lady Cynthia furiously go to work on unfastening his buttons. She pulled his trousers open, finally freeing Damian's rigid member from its confinement. He leaned back onto the couch while she caressed it with wanton exuberance. "I've never been able to do this before," she told him with an almost childlike delight.

Her touch was like fire to his senses. Rendered speechless with rapture, he willingly submitted to the whims of the impassioned lady's lust. She first took his cock tightly into her right hand, retracted his foreskin, and licked the great red head with abandon before sliding it between her parted lips. His throbbing prick had scarcely entered the lady's warm mouth before Damian could no longer hold back. His ejaculate bathed her tongue and the back of her throat while she continued to suck and milk the hot semen from his pole. A small amount oozed from the side of her mouth, but she lapped it up with her tongue when her lips began to ease away from his member. After she at last had completely withdrawn it she looked up at Damian with smiling eyes and murmured, "Thank you doctor. You may now proceed with my paroxysm."

Lady Cynthia's performance of fellatio on Damian, as with any other

service the countess purchased, was
solely about satisfying her needs.
That he might have obtained any
pleasure from it was inconsequential
to her. In fact, it was clear to
Damian that the countess never even
considered that as a possibility.
Such was the class distinction.

3 The Challenge

While   Damian   realized   physical
release, the act of fellatio continued
as a one-sided arrangement when Lady
Cynthia came to his consulting rooms
for her fortnightly sessions.   This
activity   was   entirely   for   her
pleasure, and Damian was simply being
hired by her, in confidence, to permit
her to use his cock.

   "I   find   this   to   be   a   most
satisfactory   arrangement,   doctor,"
Lady Cynthia explained. "You provide
me with an outlet which is unavailable
to   me   in   my   normal   life,   or
unthinkable   for   one   of   my   social

standing. But since you are not one of us, I may freely employ you to provide this service."

As she disappeared behind the screen to change it was not lost on Damian that he was, essentially, being looked upon in the same manner as he might consider a prostitute. That he had no control over the countess also deprived him of the pleasure usually associated with ejaculating into a warm mouth. Rather than accepting this situation for what it was, however, Lady Cynthia's attitude further fueled Damian's desire to turn the tables on her. More than merely desiring to properly fuck the countess, he wanted to have his way with her while making it clear that he was doing so. He wanted her to know that she was being used for his pleasure. Damian smiled as he set this challenge for himself. He resolved to determine a means by which he would be able to dominate her. As he sat on the couch waiting for her to change into her spanking dress, it occurred to Damian that he might be able to begin the process by exploiting her exhibitionist fetish.

"You enjoy having other look at your legs, don't you, Lady Cynthia?"

He asked innocently as she emerged.

"Indeed I do, doctor. And the arousal it provides prepares me for my subsequent spanking."

"Then might I suggest an enhancement?"

"An enhancement?" She repeated enthusiastically. "You have me intrigued, doctor."

"Stand up straight in front of me."

"Like this?" She stood attentively a few feet in front of where he was sitting, her legs pressed together.

"Lift up your dress." Damian said with an air of authority while brazenly staring at her naked knees.

Lady Cynthia's hands immediately grasped the hem and pulled it up past her waist, fully revealing her white cotton drawers which were held up by a blue ribbon. Damian slowly raised his eyes, taking in the view, then looked at her face.

"You are correct, doctor. I find lifting my dress in front of you to be most arousing." She sat next to him on the couch and reached for the buttons on his trousers. "And I will now become even more aroused," she said as she exposed and began to fondle his cock, "By enjoying your member."

Damian leaned back while Lady Cynthia's mouth descended onto his rigid rod, which had been made so by the countess following his instruction. While only an incremental victory, the door had been opened to his coercing her into more. He looked down at the beautiful brunette and successfully fought the urge to grab her head while his ejaculate exploded into her mouth.

She sucked and swallowed until satisfied that he had been sufficiently drained, then sat up again. "Button up now, doctor," she told him. "And we will proceed with my spanking."

"If it please your ladyship," Damian began as he stood up and secured his cock once again in his trousers. "Since you told be you also enjoyed being paddled, I have acquired an implement that may be similar to what you had described to me."

"Then I must see it," Lady Cynthia
said as she rose to her feet. "Is it
upstairs in your library?"

Damian closed the library door
behind them as they entered, then made
for the sideboard where the oiled
leather lay stretched out. He picked
it up, slowly drew the strap though
his fingers, doubled it, and then made
it crack by quickly pulling it tight.
While he felt a semblance of control,
he knew that was an illusion because,
in deference to their relationship,
she would have to instruct him to use
it on her. Holding the paddle across
his open hands, he asked if she would
prefer it to a spanking.

"Yes, doctor. I believe I might
enjoy that."

"Would you like to remove your
undergarments first, my lady?"

"I would like you to do that," she
responded, then lifted up the front of
her little dress. "It pleased me to
have you gaze upon my drawers
downstairs. Now I want you to look at
my legs without them on."

Damian willingly pulled on the pale blue ribbon and slid Lady Cynthia's drawers down her perfectly formed legs. She held her dress waist high as he removed the garment from around her ankles, providing him with an ample view of the soft curls surrounding the pink lips of her cunt. It was her need for exhibitionism rather than Damian's desire that was being satisfied by these actions, however.

Damian placed the drawers over the back of a chair while she made her way to the spanking horse, where he proceeded to fasten the lady's wrists on either side. "For a paddling. I will also bind your ankles," he told her, and since there was no response he proceeded to buckle them so her legs were spread wide apart. He then picked up the paddle and slowly stroked Lady Cynthia's taught spread buttocks and upper thighs, before standing to one side and delivering the first stroke. Lady Cynthia's sharp intake of air as the leather kissed her ivory bottom was eminently satisfying to Damian, but he proceeded gingerly so as to only redden but not bruise. Her writhing and the twitching

of her anal opening soon indicated
that she was close to orgasm, and
Damian wondered if he would even be
called upon to provide her paroxysm,
but through gasps she suddenly
demanded, "Now, doctor," requiring him
to toss the paddle aside and manually
attend to her. He slid the fingers of
his right hand into her now soaked
bush until they made contact with her
wanting clitoris, then began to
vibrate them from side to side. The
resulting orgasm was accompanied by
the most unladylike scream as she
violently pulled against the
restraints.

After releasing her from the horse,
Damian escorted Lady Cynthia back
downstairs to his consulting room
where she once again slid behind the
screen to resume her proper lady's
dress. "My compliments, doctor," she
told him as she left, discreetly
placing his guinea fee on the hallway
table as she passed it. "Today's
session was particularly satisfying."

Encouraged by his small victory in

having Lady Cynthia follow a simple command, Damian continued to fantasize about his growing desire to dominate her. And having her legs spread apart during the paddling, providing him with such an enticing view of her puckered anal entrance, made him realize just how he wanted to go about it. He concluded that the perfect way to dominate Lady Cynthia would be to bugger her. It would be necessary, of course, to have her feel it was to her benefit that she submit to him. Damian smiled to himself. He had an idea.

4 Role Play

Sitting on the couch after her next session, Lady Cynthia confided to Damian that she found herself fantasizing while undergoing the treatment, then added, "Although I admit to feeling rather awkward in admitting this to you, doctor."

"In spite of conventional wisdom preaching to the contrary, I tell my patients that fantasizing is both quite natural and healthy. What was it that you were fantasizing about?"

"In my mind I was witnessing the housemaid being brought to climax while Joseph, the butler, was having his way with her."

"As in the dreams you told me about previously?"

"The same." Lady Cynthia nodded slowly.

"And you are still experiencing these dreams, then, Lady Cynthia?"

"They do persist, yes. And, inexplicably, they have become even more vivid of late."

"Why do you think that may be?"

"I cannot fathom it. It had made sense that satisfying my need to perform fellatio should have curbed them, but instead, my doing so appears to have increased their intensity." She turned to Damian. "Why should that be?"

"I suspect, my lady, it is because that, rather than satisfying your desire, performing fellatio has served to bring you closer to realizing what it truly is that you really want."

Lady Cynthia slowly shook her head. "It vexes me terribly to be unable to grasp the nature of my own desires, doctor." She looked at Damian with wide eyes. "Is there anything you can do for me?"

"Of course," Damian answered reassuringly. "As a physician, my focus is directed towards the psyche of my patients. And as such I have taken much interest in a new field of study which is being called psychiatry. Used in this discipline is a technique called role play, which I am confident can serve to answer your question."

"Role play?"

"It is a process which enables a physician and patient to explore the fantasy together. Once they understand it, they can them move to achieve a successful resolution."

"How curious. How does role play work?"

"Quite simply, the patient acts out her fantasies as if she were an actress playing a role. In your case, if you wish it, we could re-create an interaction between you, as the maid, and Joseph. By working through it thus, we may learn what it is that disturbs you so."

"I would then, in this manner, be permitted to do what Lucy did?" Lady Cynthia covered her mouth with her right hand, feigning shock, but the expression in her eyes betrayed that she was hiding a smile.

"Consider it in the same manner as a clinically induced paroxysm is not considered a sexual orgasm. Physician directed role play is, after all, a medical procedure."

The countess regained her composure. "And you would be willing to play the role of Joseph for me?" She asked. "I believe I have provide you with sufficient detail as to what is to transpire."

"Certainly. I will dress for and act the part. I will also provide you with a maid's uniform and create a scenario where you may freely become Lucy."

"Then I wish to experience this role play as soon as possible, doctor. When may we re-convene?"

Damian walked to the desk to consult his calendar. I am free all of Thursday afternoon," he said as he looked up. "Two days from now?"

"Splendid."

The countess arrived promptly at 1pm the following Thursday afternoon and Damian beckoned her to a chair in front of his desk while he sat behind it. "You must understand that once you we begin the role play, you will have become Lucy and will be treated accordingly." He looked directly at her as he spoke. "You will no longer have the authority of a countess until the role play has concluded."

Lady Cynthia nodded slowly. "I understand."

"Behind the screen you will find a maid's uniform dress. When I leave the room you are to change into it, remove all of your jewelry and take down your hair. You will then proceed upstairs to one of the guest rooms where I, as the butler, will be waiting for you. You will know which room because I will leave the door ajar. By entering the room and closing the door behind you, you will indicate you have agreed to become

Lucy, and we shall then engage in the role play." He placed both hands on the desktop and stood up. "Do you have any questions, my lady?"

Lady Cynthia's lips began to quiver, fluttering between excitement and trepidation, but she managed to eke out, "No questions, doctor." Her fingers nervously intertwining in her lap, she turned to quietly watch Damian exit the room. As soon as he had closed the door behind him, however, she excitedly leaped to her feet and scurried behind the screen while removing the carefully placed combs from her hair. She quickly stripped off her dress and took off her jewelry, then dressed herself in the black and white maid uniform. There was something incredibly erotic about wearing it; perhaps it was the anticipation of what she hoped would be transpiring. For the first time in her life she was not going to be required to act like a lady.

Damian, in the meantime, was donning a butler's livery in order to become 'Joseph' in a guest room, after which he set the door ajar and sat at the small table, to wait for 'Lucy' to arrive.

'Lucy' gingerly closed the door and stood with her back against it while 'Joseph' rose from his chair and, his eyes seeming to beam with delight, approached her. He slid his arm around her waist and gave her a kiss on her cheek while coaxing her towards the table. "What do you think of this position, Lucy?" He whispered as her eyes alighted on the picture in the open book. It was of a woman reclining with her dress pulled up and her legs spread.

"I think you're a naughty man, Joseph." She slid her hand across his pants. "And I also think that looking at this picture has made you as stiff as a rolling pin."

"Oh, it's having you here with me that's done that," he replied, knocking the book off the table as he scrambled to sit in the chair and pull 'Lucy' onto his knee. He slid his hand under her dress and ravenously kissed her.

'Lucy' eagerly returned 'Joseph's' kisses while proceeding to unbutton 'Joseph's' pants. Successful, she released and squeezed his truncheon. "Do you want my knickers off now, Joseph?" She panted.

"Don't be impatient, lass," Joseph responded teasingly. "You know you must ask me nicely for it first."

'Lucy' made no resistance as 'Joseph' pushed her down her onto her knees and fondled her breasts while pulling the uniform off her shoulders in order to pin her arms to her sides. She watched, wide-eyed, as he placed the glistening purple head of his cock just inches in front of her face. Then, obediently opening her mouth, she began to give it a most luscious sucking while he entwined his fingers into her hair. His hands on her head thus, 'Joseph' manipulated 'Lucy's' back and forth movements, pushing himself further and further into her mouth until she succumbed to an involuntary gag. "There's a good girl," he told her, withdrawing his member while she regained her breath. "You've asked nicely, so now you have your fuck."

With a gentle effort, 'Joseph' eased 'Lucy' to her feet, reclined her backwards on the couch, raised up her

dress and pulled her undergarments
off. She did not flinch from the
position he placed her in, which was
providing him a full view of her
splendid white legs. What riveted his
gaze, though, were the pouting lips of
her cunt; surprisingly wet and
slightly parted in a most inviting
manner. He grabbed her ankles and
pulled her legs wide apart as he
positioned himself on his knees
between them. Then bringing his shaft
to the entrance of the gaping crack,
he rammed it right in.

'Lucy' gasped and immediately
enveloped 'Joseph' with both arms and
threw her legs around his buttocks.
Holding onto him tightly, she heaved
her bottom up and down while 'Joseph'
pounded in and out. Their movements
became more and more furious until
they suddenly froze in a jointly
spasmodic embrace, which then melted
into a lethargy of post-coital
enjoyment as they lay on the couch
together.

'Joseph' was first to break the
silence. "You'd better get back to
your duties now, Lucy," he said as he
withdrew his instrument from her hot

cunt and sat up.

"Not yet," she responded playfully. She sat next to him and reached for his cock, which was now reduced in size and all slimy with her juices. She gave 'Joseph' a kiss on his lips while she massaged his limp affair, then slid to her knees on the floor before him.

'Joseph's' face flushed with pleasure as 'Lucy' took his instrument once again into her mouth and soon had it restored it to its prior stiffness. He gasped, grabbed the sides of her head, and held her in place while he realized a second ejaculation into her mouth. "Ah, you know what I like, don't you lass." He laughed contentedly as he eased 'Lucy' to her feet.

"I had to give you a good suck after the exquisite pleasure you had given me," she responded.

"And a good one it was, to be sure, Lucy." He patted her bottom. "But since you've got me nicely spent, I think you'd best be on your way now."

Damian slowly dressed back into his physician's suit and waited to give Lady Cynthia time to recover and compose herself before he went back downstairs, still smiling from the role play. But seeing her sitting upright on the couch, once again wearing her elaborate clothing and adorned with her jewelry, immediately snapped him back into his proper role. "There you are, doctor," she said in a crisp tone. "I must say that Lucy is certainly a lively girl."

"Certainly," he agreed "It is often said of the lower classes that they enjoy a lust for life, my lady. And that they have no reservations about the pleasures of sexual activity."

"And in that regard, they have an advantage over those of us who have it instilled to repress such things."

Damian poured two glasses of sherry and gave one to his client. "Now that you have experienced being Lucy, do you find you better understand what it is inside you that torments you in your dreams?"

"I do." The countess sipped her sherry as she attempted to compose exactly what she wanted to say. "In the butler-maid relationship, it seems that Lucy accepts that she is in a subservient position to Joseph. And, curiously, it is through him deriving his pleasure that she derives hers." She quickly drained her glass. "It was incredibly arousing when Joseph pushed her to her knees and made her perform fellatio. I never imagined that being forced could be so erotic, and the orgasm from the subsequent intercourse came almost instantly. The only thing remaining to do after that was for her to swallow his semen, and she did that to please him as much as her."

"Then I conclude that the role play has been a success, my lady. For you have discovered what your true desires are."

"Quite so. In every aspect of my life I am the countess in control of all that surrounds me. But when it comes to sexual activities I appear to have a desperate need to relinquish that control."

"And that knowledge should now serve to placate your dreams."

"But what of my real life, doctor?

Now knowing what it is that I truly desire, I fear a future of torment since I do not possess the means to act on it." Lady Cynthia's composure had left her; she was speaking to him from the heart. "My sexual relations with the earl consist of requisite intercourse every few weeks, during which I am to lie still and remain silent. The only orgasm I experience is when I am treated in your consulting rooms." Her eyes looked directly at Damian. "I dare say that today's role play was the first time I have experienced such passion, but then I was only playing a role." She raised her hands and her head shook rapidly from side to side.

Damian refilled her glass and offered it to her to help her calm down.

"Thank you, doctor," she said, taking the glass and quaffing half of it. "Your wonderful role play showed me what I want, but it wasn't real. It wasn't me being myself."

Damian now knew that he had her, but suppressed his delight. "Would you really want that, Lady Cynthia?" He responded calmly. "All we have explored has been for diagnostic purposes, which still remains purely in the clinical realm. Are you really implying," he said with feigned astonishment, "That you would consider actually acting on your fantasy?"

"Please do not judge me harshly, doctor. But I fear that I must."

Damian shook his head. "A lady of your standing would be putting herself at considerable risk by acting in such a manner. You would be required to find a discreet partner with whom you had a considerable amount of trust."

"Oh, do not be coy, doctor. You know that you are the only man I could turn to."

"But I am your physician, my lady."

"Couldn't you also be my lover?"

"I'm afraid not, for that would violate my physician's oath."

Lady Cynthia began to chuckle. "Doctor Thatch," she began, slowly shaking her head. "If you would acquiesce to my request, I would surely no longer have need for your services as a physician."

Damian took a deep, thoughtful breath as he refilled their glasses. "There is no question that I find you most desirable, Lady Cynthia, and I would greatly enjoy such a relationship with you." He looked directly at her. "But it would require that we dispense with class distinction." He took a drink, his eyes affixed on hers. "And since we have learned of your orientation towards sexual submission, I am inclined to agree to your request only if you agree to become submissive to me."

"What, precisely, would that entail?"

"In a word, obedience." Damian walked over to his desk and produced from the top drawer a book by the Marquis De Sade he had already selected for her. "Study this book," he said as he handed it to her. "Then tell me if any of the scenarios presented therein appeal to you. Unless you advise me otherwise, we will discuss it further at your next scheduled appointment."

"Which will not," she added, cocking her head slightly to the left.

51

"Be an actual physician appointment?"

"If you do elect to keep that appointment," he told her. "It will most certainly not be."

5 Fantasies Fulfilled

The day before Lady Cynthia's
fortnightly appointment a package was
delivered to Damian at his office. It
contained the book he had loaned to
the countess. A folded paper had been
inserted as a bookmark and the words
'Thank you, Cyn,' were written on it.
He opened to the referenced page and
broke into a wide smile. The fantasy
that Lady Cynthia had shared was most
consistent with his desires, and she
had even provided her submissive
moniker. This would be fantasy
fulfillment, not a role play. Cyn was
Lady Cynthia's inner, secret self, and
Damian was about to have his way with
her.

She arrived precisely at the appointed time, and as soon as Rosie had shown her into his office Damian silently beckoned for Lady Cynthia to go behind the screen to transform into her alter-ego. She quickly emerged, wearing the short sailor dress, ankle socks and patent leather shoes. Damian unabashedly looked up and down her body as she stood attentively in the middle of the room, paying particular interest to her naked knees and calves. "Tell me your name," he demanded.

"My name is Cyn, sir." She looked down at her shoes as she answered.

"Well, Cyn. I am going to take upstairs to my study where I will expect your obedience." He hooked his index finger under her chin so he could speak directly to her face. "Be a good girl for me and I will provide you with the release you crave."

"I hope I am able please you, sir." The words coming from her quivering lips were almost whispers, but her underlying excitement was evident when she added, "I will do whatever you want," with a coy smile.

Damian closed the door to his library behind him and told Cyn to stand in front of him while he settled into a leather armchair. It suited him admirably that she had an exhibitionist fetish. Since the first time she came into his office he had lusted to see her naked body, but it had never been appropriate as a physician to have a countess completely undress. Now, however, since she was now Cyn, he was going to have her strip. "Raise the front of your dress up," he instructed. His cock began to strain against the restraint of his trousers as he watched her immediately comply, holding up the hem to fully reveal her pastel lace undergarment. "Now remove your drawers."

"Yes, sir."

"Hand them to me."

Quickly stepping out of the garment that had dropped to her ankles after she untied the blue ribbon which held them up, Cyn presented them to Damian

with her outstretched right hand. He
nodded, folded them up, and placed it
on the floor next to his chair. He
leaned forward, placed both hands on
the sides of her knees, and then
slowly moved his hands up the sides of
Cyn's legs, pushing her dress up as he
did so. "Hold your dress up this
high," he told her once the perfect
curly triangle was in his full view.

Cyn's trembling hands gripped
tightly onto the fabric, but she
remained still while Damian stroked
her labia lips with the back of his
right index finger. "Legs apart," he
told her without looking up, then slid
two fingers between her thighs as she
did so. Her cunt was soaked. He
smiled and sat back in his chair.
"Take off your dress."

Cyn pulled the dress over her head
and handed it to Damian who, without
taking his eyes off her, folded it
neatly and placed it on the floor next
to her underwear. He was finally able
to admire her perfect body as she
posed with her hands behind her back
in front of him. His eyes went to her
lily white breasts and he reached out
to tease each of the chestnut nipples
which adorned them. The straining in

his pants preventing him from delaying more, however, so he leaned back in his chair and began to unfasten his trousers. "You will now please me with your mouth," he told her. "I want you on your knees."

"Yes, sir," Cyn eagerly replied as she knelt in front of Damian. No sooner had he produced his pulsing rigidity than she leaned forward and took his glistening bulb into her mouth. Damian's hands stroked her hair in encouragement as she slid his cock in and out while simultaneously stimulating it with her tongue. It took only minutes before he felt pulsing sensations, and although he attempted to delay the inevitable in order to prolong the delight of the pre-ejaculation sensation, he soon involuntarily gripped her head to hold it in place while he flooded into Cyn's mouth. "Swallow," he ordered, gasping between breaths of satisfaction. "And continue sucking until I tell you to stop."

Guided by his hands in her hair, Cyn willingly complied with Damian's instructions until he permitted her mouth to ease away from his now more limber instrument. "Good girl," he told her as he fastened up his pants, prompting a beaming smile. His words, telling her that she had pleased him, were a reward in themselves.

Buttoned up, Damian then stood up, took Cyn's hands in his, and eased her to her feet. "We're now going to the spanking horse," he said. "Where I'm going to tie you down and thoroughly redden that bottom of yours."

Cyn willingly lay across the horse, her arms hanging from each side, while Damian attached the leather restraints to her wrists. He then proceeded behind her, ordered her to spread her legs, and secured her ankles such that they were eighteen inches part. With his right hand he caressed and then squeezed each of her buttocks, then slipped his hand between her thighs and ran his middle finger between her parted labia lips, eliciting a moan of delight from her. "It's time for your spanking," he teased, then brought his now moist hand down onto her left buttock. The simultaneous sounds of slaps along with Cyn's gasping was pure ecstasy for Damian as his

continued ministrations revived his
member to its former rigidity. Cyn's
bottom and the backs of her upper
thighs were soon turned to an evenly
spread rouge, both her genital and
anal areas began twitching
involuntarily, and her gasps had
transitioned into guttural sighs.
Damian reached out and touched her
inflamed clitoris with the tip of his
index finger, prompting a plea of,
"Please, sir."

"Please?" Damian asked teasingly.
"Would you like to ask me for
something?"

"Please, sir," she repeated.
"Please bring me to release."

Damian dragged his fingertip
between the lips of her cunt to
moisten it, then began to inscribe
small circles around her puckered anal
entrance. "I am only too happy to
provide you with release, Cyn," he
told her, his finger now entering her
bottom hole. "But I want to do
something to you first." His index
finger had now penetrated an inch and
her muscles were spasmodically
squeezing it. "Can you guess what it
is that I want?"

"You." She swallowed hard, then blurted out, "You want to bugger me."

"That's right." He removed his finger, then re-inserted it along with his middle finger. "All you have to do is ask me to do it."

"Please, sir." Cyn pulled against the restraints and tried to wriggle, forcing Damian's two fingers deeper inside. "Please bugger me."

"As you wish." Damian held his cock, hardened with anticipation, in his left hand, and applied a generous amount of spit to the glistening bulbous head with his right. He then placed it against the entrance to Cyn's bottom and slowly leaned towards her. The resulting cry emanating from her mouth was a combination of pleasure and pain. Damian grasped her hips and remained in that position until her sphincter eased its grip, backed out a little, then pushed two inches further in. Cyn's cries suggested that she was beginning to derive more pleasure than pain from this invasion of her virgin anus, encouraging Damian to begin to slowly pump in and out. Four strokes later he was fully inserted. He remained still with his lower torso resting against her hot buttocks and reached his right hand around her front to gently tease her clitoris. "I'll bring you to orgasm when I am finished with you," he said, then resumed his tight grip on her hips. He pulled half way out, then slammed back, eliciting a scream of, "Fuck my bottom," from an on-the-edge Cyn.

No further encouragement required, Damian proceeded to achieve what he had wanted for so long. He selfishly pounded into Cyn's bottom until his pulsating cock delivered the last of his semen deep into her bowels.

After slowly withdrawing, Damian silently dressed himself and then unfastened the restraints. "You've pleased me well," he told Cyn as he helped her to stand. "So now you will have your reward."

He stood her next to the couch, laid her dress down on it, and instructed her to sit in the middle, on top of her garment. Then, standing at one end, he placed his hands on her shoulders, and eased her back so she was lying down with her head resting on the settee arm.

"Keep your left foot on the floor," Damian said as he grasped her right ankle and picked it up. "You're going to spread your legs wide apart for me."

Damian placed Cyn's right foot onto the back of the settee and positioned himself sitting between them. The humiliation of being exposed this way was so arousing for the exhibitionist Cyn that it took only a touch of Damian's finger onto her clitoris before she exploded into a violent orgasm. Her head thrashed from side to side and her fingers dug into the fabric of the couch while Damian persisted, delivering her into a series of four consecutive spasms before her body wilted, satiated, onto the couch. Damian withdrew his hand and continued to gaze at her naked body until her eyes fluttered and she was recovered sufficiently to sit up again. "Wine?" he asked rhetorically as he rose and proceeded to the small table to pour out two glasses.

The Countess Cynthia no longer
visits Dr. Damian Thatch since she no
longer suffers from hysteria or
anxiety. Cyn does continue to visit
the dominant Damian, however, and
willingly submits to his wishes
several times each year.

Dorian Shellan

Get All the Books in the Series at VictorianStories.com

Printed in Great Britain
by Amazon